Have NO FEAR, for GOD is NEAR!

Aaron Zaretsky
illustrated by **Brenda DeVries**

To my daughter Leah.
When you were little and had nightmares,
I comforted you with the words,

"Have no fear, for God is near."

And to my grandchildren:
Aviva, Judah, Ari, Tovah, Everley, Wren,
and all others who may come after you.
Make Jesus your superhero, and have no fear.

Special thanks to John Cameron, Rob and Carolyn Covell, and Kimberly Love
whose love and support have helped make this book a reality.

- Aaron Zaretsky

To the Forerunners,
to the Young Lions of RSAI,
and to the Pioneers.
Be strong and courageous.
Do not be afraid to take the land.

- Brenda DeVries

Have No Fear, for God is Near!

Cover art, illustrations, and book design by Brenda DeVries - INSTAGRAM: @aria.echo
God's hero suit original design by Judah Zaretsky

First published in the United States in 2024
by Amazon Kindle Direct Publishing

ISBN 9798322997610

A Note to the Parents

At sixteen, fear was still a big part of my life. Then Jesus came in, and my fears began to disappear. Psalm 34:4 became my reality. God kept His promise to deliver me from all my fears.

The purpose of this book is to acknowledge that children's fears are real and should be taken seriously, and dealt with quickly. Offering validation, comfort, and reassurance that God is with them empowers them to face their fears with courageous confidence.

This book also aims to teach children about God's love, and how it applies to every area of our lives. Just as the Bible has stories of ordinary people overcoming fear through their faith in an extraordinary God, sharing your own stories of God helping you deal with fear can also build children's trust.

And finally, it seeks family unity as the foundation for nurturing and affirming children. The goal is to support them to confidently make good choices as they step into their destinies, driven by faith and not fear.

Aaron Zaretsky

When you are all alone
and you hear noises in your home,

Have **NO FEAR,**
for **GOD** is **NEAR!**

When it is dark so much
that you feel a monster
will eat you up,

Have **NO FEAR,** for **GOD** is **NEAR!**

When you are watching TV
and you see something
so-o-o-o-o scary,

Have **NO FEAR,** for **GOD** is **NEAR!**

When you're sick at night,
and you don't feel too right,

Have **NO FEAR,** for **GOD** is **NEAR!**

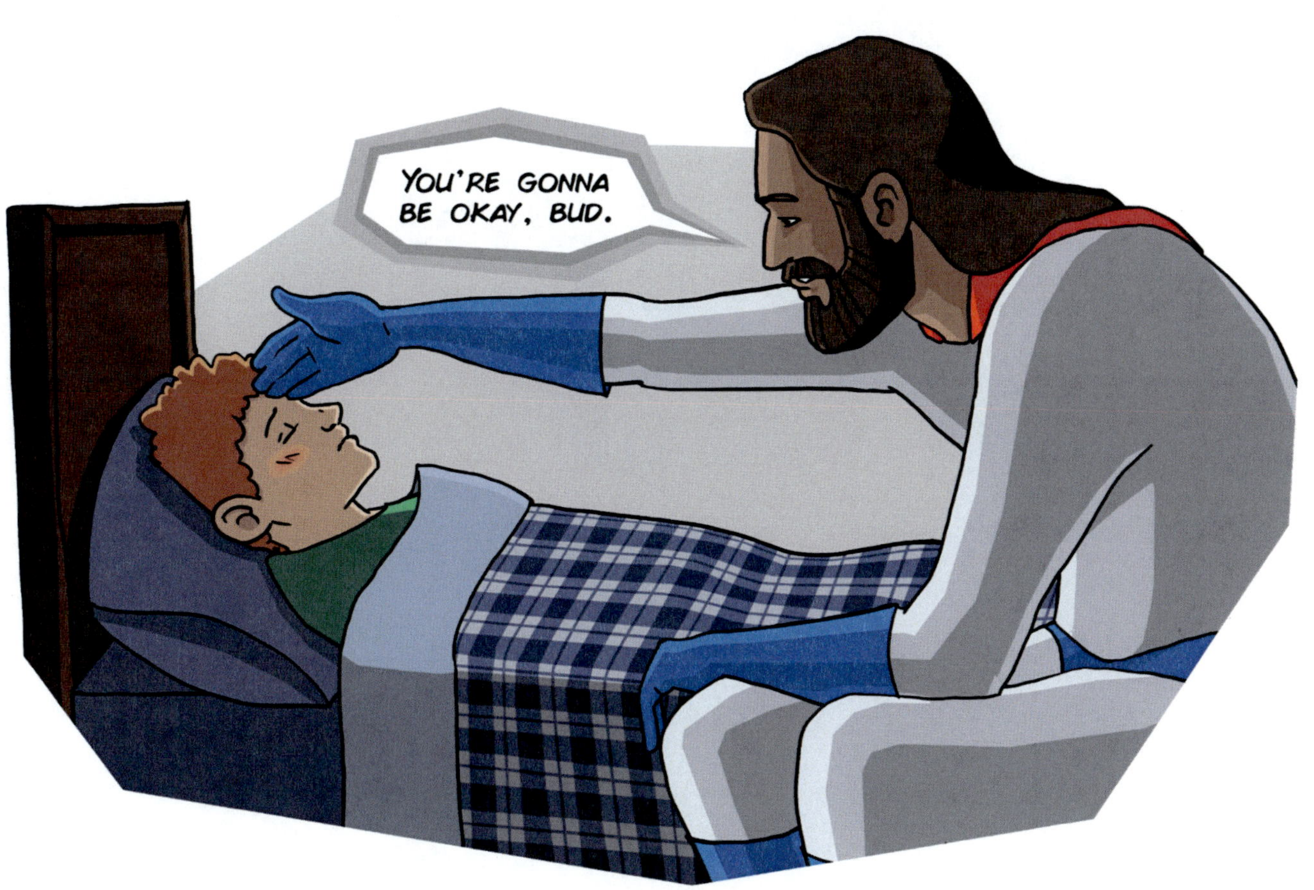

When a doctor helps you heal
by giving you a big, bigggggg needle,

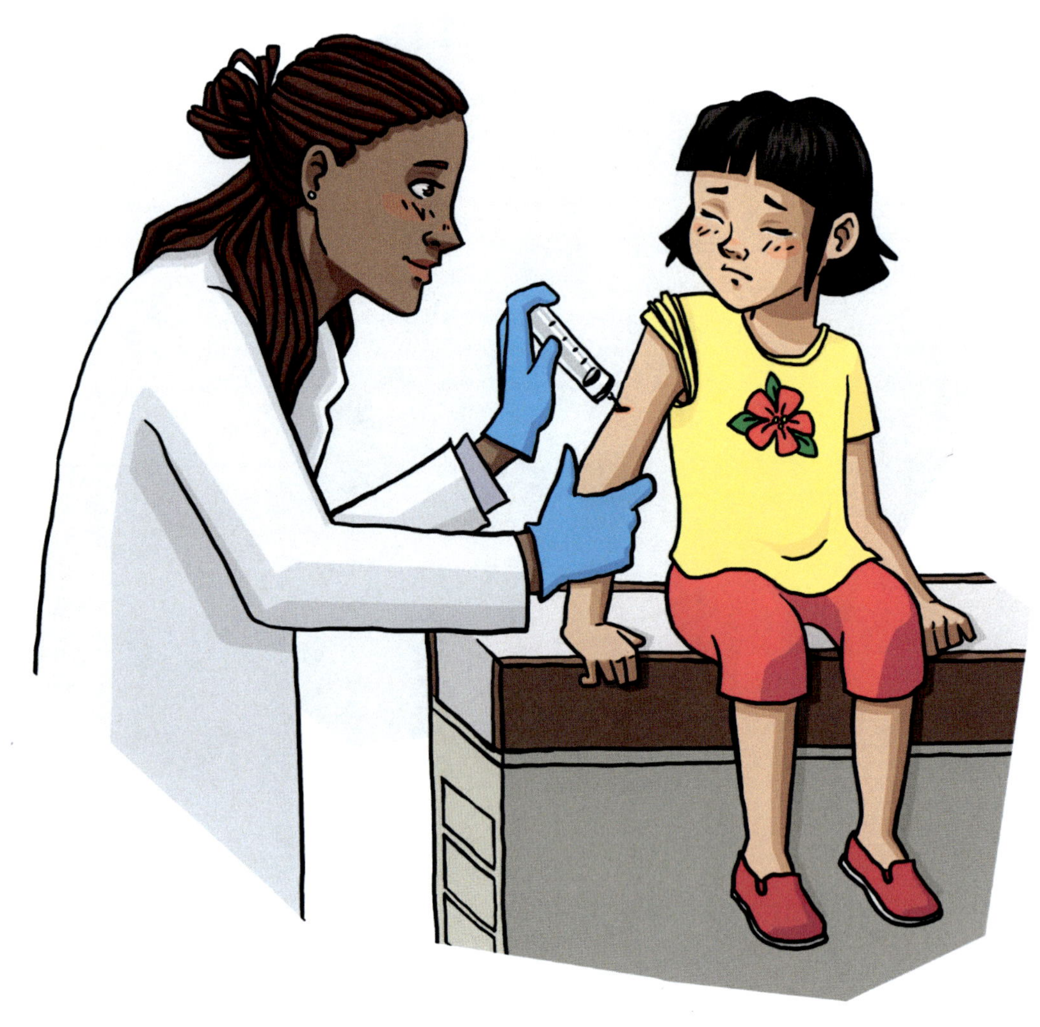

Have **NO FEAR,** for **GOD** is **NEAR!**

When you're
feeling mad,

and you're
feeling so bad,

or you are
just feeling sad,

Have **NO FEAR**, for **GOD** is **NEAR**!

When you're shopping with your mom,
and you are running along,

then you
look around,
and she is
nowhere
to be found,

Have *NO FEAR*,
for *GOD* is *NEAR*!

When your parents are mad
because you did something bad,

Have *NO FEAR*, for *GOD* is *NEAR!*

When your home is very far,
and you don't know where you are,

Have **NO FEAR,** for **GOD** is **NEAR!**

When you're at camp
and it gets cold and damp,

Have ***NO FEAR,*** for ***GOD*** is ***NEAR!***

When you first go to school
to learn the golden rule,

Have *NO FEAR*,
for *GOD* is *NEAR!*

When you have a test
and you hope to do your best,

Have **NO FEAR,** for **GOD** is **NEAR!**

When something for you
is very hard to do,

Have **NO FEAR,** for **GOD** is **NEAR!**

When you want to pray
but you don't know what to say,

Have ***NO FEAR,*** for ***GOD*** is ***NEAR!***

Because God knows you
and He loves you true,

I have **NO FEAR,** for **GOD** is **NEAR!**

Made in the USA
Middletown, DE
28 January 2025